THE AMERICAN GIRLS

17  *74*

FELICITY, a spunky, spritely colonial girl,
full of energy and independence

18 *24*

JOSEFINA, an Hispanic girl whose heart and
hopes are as big as the New Mexico sky

18  *54*

KIRSTEN, a pioneer girl of strength and
spirit who settles on the frontier

18  *64*

ADDY, a courageous girl determined to be
free in the midst of the Civil War

19  *04*

SAMANTHA, a bright Victorian beauty, an
orphan raised by her wealthy grandmother

19  *34*

KIT, a clever, resourceful girl facing the
Great Depression with spirit and determination

19  *44*

MOLLY, who schemes and dreams on the
home front during World War Two

1824
MEET JOSEFINA
An American Girl

SCHOLASTIC INC.

New York   Toronto   London   Auckland   Sydney
Mexico City   New Delhi   Hong Kong   Buenos Aires

American Girl®

ISBN   0-439-39218-7

12 11 10 9 8 7 6 5 4 3 2   2 3 4 5 6 7/0

Printed in the U.S.A   23

First Scholastic printing, February 2002

PICTURE CREDITS
The following individuals and organizations have generously given permission to reprint illustrations contained in "Looking Back": p. 76—*Don Pedro de Peralta surveying the site for Santa Fe in 1610.* Painting by Roy Grinnell. Courtesy Sunwest Bank of Santa Fe and Roy Grinnell; p. 77—*Las quebradoras,* artist unknown (19th century), Museo Nacional de Historia, Mexico City; p. 78—Photos by John MacLean. Artifacts from a private collection; *El fandango mexicano* (El jarave), Hesiquio Iriarte; p. 79—Cat. #42247/12 San Juan Moccasins. Blair Clark photo. Museum of Indian Arts & Culture/Laboratory of Anthropology, Santa Fe, New Mexico; Photo by Ben Wittick, courtesy Museum of New Mexico, neg. 56120 (pueblo); p. 80—Photograph by Michael Freeman from *ADOBE* by Orlando Romero and David Larkin. Compilation copyright © 1994 by David Larkin. Reprinted by permission of Houghton Mifflin Company. All rights reserved. (courtyard); p. 81—From the collections of the Millicent A. Rogers Museum, Taos, New Mexico. BL65. (blue blanket); The Spanish Colonial Arts Society, Inc. Collection on loan to the Museum of New Mexico at the Museum of International Folk Art, Santa Fe (red blanket, white blanket); arqueta, 18th century, Olinala, Guerrero, from the collection of the Museo de Franz Mayer, Mexico City (trunk); The Brooklyn Museum, Museum Collection Fund and the Dick S. Ramsay Fund (dishes); photos © 1996 by Jack Parsons. Items from the collection of The Spanish Colonial Arts Society (necklace, hair comb); p. 82—Image by Josiah Gregg, *Commerce of the Prairies,* University of Oklahoma Press (mule train); *Dragon,* Claudio Linati, in *Trajes Civiles, Militares y Religiosos de Mexico (1828).*

Edited by Peg Ross
Designed by Mark Macauley, Myland McRevey, Laura Moberly, and Jane S. Varda
Art Directed by Jane S. Varda
Cover Art by Jean-Paul Tibbles

TO MY HUSBAND, MICHAEL
AND MY DAUGHTER, KATHERINE
WITH LOVE

Josefina and her family speak
Spanish, so you'll see some
Spanish words in this book.
If you can't tell what a word
means from reading the story
or looking at the illustrations,
you can turn to the "Glossary
of Spanish Words" that begins
on page 84. It will tell you what
the word means and how to
pronounce it.

Remember that in Spanish,
"j" is pronounced like "h."
That means Josefina's name is
pronounced "ho-seh-FEE-nah."

Table of Contents

Josefina's Family

Chapter One
Primroses   1

Chapter Two
Abuelito's Surprise   19

Chapter Three
A Gift for Tía Dolores   41

Chapter Four
Josefina's Idea   56

Looking Back   75

Glossary of Spanish Words   84

PAPÁ
*Josefina's father, who
guides his family
and his rancho with
quiet strength.*

ANA
*Josefina's oldest sister,
who is married and has
two little boys.*

JOSEFINA
*A nine-year-old girl
whose heart and hopes
are as big as the
New Mexico sky.*

FRANCISCA
*Josefina's fifteen-year-old
sister, who is headstrong
and impatient.*

CLARA
*Josefina's practical,
sensible sister, who is
twelve years old.*

ABUELITO
*Josefina's loving
grandfather,
a trader who leads
caravans to Mexico.*

TÍA DOLORES
*Josefina's aunt, who
has lived far away in
Mexico City for ten years.*

CHAPTER
ONE
—

PRIMROSES

Josefina Montoya hummed to herself as she stood in the sunshine waiting for her sisters. It was a bright, breezy morning in late summer and the girls were going to the stream to wash clothes. Josefina's basket was full of laundry to be washed, but she didn't mind. She enjoyed going to the stream on a day like this. The sky was a deep, strong blue. Josefina wished she could touch it. She was sure it would feel smooth and cool.

Josefina liked to stand just in front of her house, where the life of her papá's *rancho* was going on all around her. From here, she could smell the sharp scent of smoke from the kitchen fire. She could see cows and sheep grazing in the pastures. Yellow grass rolled all the way to the dark green trees on the foothills of the mountains, and the mountains zigzagged up to the sky. She could hear all the sounds of the rancho: chickens clucking, donkeys braying, dogs barking, birds chirping, workers hammering, and someone laughing. The sounds seemed like music to Josefina. The wind joined in the music when it rustled the leaves on the cottonwood trees. And always, under it all, was the murmur of the stream.

Josefina shaded her eyes. Even from this far away, she could see Papá. He sat very straight and tall on his horse. He was talking to the workers in the cornfield near the stream. The rancho had belonged to Papá's family for more than one hundred years. All those years, Papá's family had cared for the animals and the land. It was not an easy life. Everyone had to work hard. Some years there was plenty of rain so that the crops grew and the animals were healthy. Some years there was not enough rain. Then the soil was dry and the animals went thirsty. But through good times and bad the

rancho went on. It provided everything Josefina
and her family needed to live. It gave them food,
clothing, and shelter. Josefina loved the rancho. It
was her home. She believed that it was the most
beautiful place in all of New Mexico and all of
the world.

Josefina was dancing a little dance of impatience
to go with the song she was humming when her
oldest sister, Ana, came outside to join her.

"Josefina," Ana said. "You remind me of a little
bird, singing and hopping from one foot to the other
like that."

"If I were a bird," said Josefina with a grin,
"I could have flown to the stream and back twenty
times by now. I've been waiting and waiting for you!
Where are Francisca and Clara?"

Ana sighed. "They're coming," she said. "They
couldn't agree on whose turn it was to carry the
washing tub."

Josefina and Ana looked at each other and
shook their heads. They got along beautifully.
But Francisca and Clara, the middle sisters, often
disagreed. It was always over some silly little thing.
They reminded Josefina of goats she had seen

ramming into each other head-to-head for no particular reason.

When the girls appeared at last, it was easy to see who had won the argument. Francisca, looking pleased with herself, carried only a basket of laundry balanced on her head. Clara, looking cross, carried the large copper washing tub.

Josefina put her basket into the copper tub. "I'll take one handle of the tub, Clara," she said. "We'll carry it between us."

Clara said, *"Gracias."* But she sounded more grumpy than grateful.

Josefina knew a way to cheer her up. "Let's race to the stream!" she said.

"Oh, no . . ." Francisca began to say. She didn't like to do anything that might muss her clothes or her hair.

But Josefina and Clara had already taken off running, so Ana and Francisca had to run, too.

The sisters flew down the dirt path that sloped past the fruit trees, past the fields, and to the stream. Josefina and Clara reached the stream first, plunked the tub down, kicked off their moccasins, and ran into the shallow water. Then they turned and

"Let's race to the stream!" Josefina said.

scooped up handfuls of water to splash Ana and Francisca, who shrieked with laughter as the water hit them.

"Stop!" cried Francisca. She held up her basket to shield her face.

"Now, girls," Ana scolded gently. "We've come to wash the clothes that are in our baskets, *not* the ones we're wearing!"

Josefina and Clara stopped splashing. They were out of breath anyway. They filled the copper tub with water from the stream. Josefina knelt next to the tub. She took the root of a yucca plant out of the little leather pouch she wore at her waist and then pounded it between two rocks. The shredded yucca root made a nice lather of soapy bubbles in the water.

yucca root

Josefina put a dirty shirt in the tub and scrubbed it all over. Then she swooshed it around in the stream to rinse out the soap.

The sun was hot on her head and her back, and the water was cool on her arms and hands. Josefina liked to think about how the water started out as snow on the mountaintops. It melted and flowed all the way down to this little pool in the stream without ever losing its cool freshness. She knew that it was water that brought life to the rancho. Water from the stream was channeled into ditches so that it would flow through the fields. Without water, nothing would grow.

Josefina twisted the shirt to wring it out, and watched drops of water fall back into the stream and go on their way. Then she carefully spread the shirt on top of a bush.

"The sun and the breeze will dry the clothes quickly today," she said as she washed some socks.

"Yes," agreed Ana. "Mamá would have said, 'You see, girls? God has sent us a good drying day. Monday is laundry day even in heaven.'"

"And then Mamá would have said, 'Pull your *rebozos* up to shade your faces, girls. You don't want your skin to look like old leather!'" added Francisca, who was always careful of her skin.

The sisters laughed softly together and then grew quiet. Speaking of their mamá always made them thoughtful. Mamá had died a little more than a year ago. The

rebozo

sorrow of her death was always in their hearts.

7

Josefina looked at the stream flowing past and listened to its low, rushing sound. Since Mamá died she had learned a truth that was both bitter and sweet. She had learned that love does not end. Josefina would always love Mamá, and so she would always miss her.

Josefina knew her sisters were also thinking about Mamá because Francisca said, "Look. See those yellow flowers across the stream?" She pointed with a soapy hand. "Aren't they evening primroses? They're in the shade, so they haven't wilted yet this morning. Mamá used to love those flowers."

"Yes, she did," said Clara, agreeing with Francisca for once. "Why don't you pick some, Josefina? You could dry them and put them in your memory box."

"All right," said Josefina. Papá had given her a little wooden box of Mamá's. Josefina called it her memory box because in it she kept small things that reminded her of Mamá, such as a piece of Mamá's favorite lavender-scented soap. The box had been made by Josefina's great-great-grandfather. On its top there was a carving of the sun coming up over the

highest mountain and shining on the rancho just
the way Josefina saw it rise every morning.

The quickest, driest way to the primroses was
to walk across a fallen log that made a narrow bridge
over the stream. Josefina climbed up onto the log.
She held her arms out for balance and began to
walk across.

"Oh, do be careful," warned Ana. Because she
was the oldest sister, Ana had become a motherly
worrier since Mamá died.

Josefina did not think of herself as a brave
person at all. She was afraid of snakes and lightning
and guns, and shy of people she didn't know. But
she wasn't afraid of crossing the log, which wasn't
very high above the stream anyway. She walked
across, picked the primroses, and tucked the stems
in her pouch. She let the yellow flowers stick out
so that they wouldn't be crushed. On the
way back, she decided to tease Ana
to make her laugh. She pretended
to lose her balance. She waved her
arms wildly up and down and
wobbled more and more with
each step.

primroses in pouch

"Josefina Montoya!" said Ana, who saw that she was fooling. "How can you be so shy and sweet in company when you're so playful with your sisters? You tease the life out of me. You'll make me old before my time!"

"You sound just like our grandfather," said Josefina as she jumped to the ground.

She pretended to talk like Abuelito. "Yes, yes, yes, my beautiful granddaughters! This was the finest trip I've ever made! Oh, the adventures, the adventures! But this was my last trip. Oh, how these trips age me! They make me—"

"—old before my time!" all the sisters sang out together. Abuelito said the same thing after every journey.

Abuelito was their mamá's father. He was a trader, and once each year he organized a huge caravan. The caravan was made up of many carts pulled by oxen and many mules carrying packs. The carts and the mules were loaded with wool, hides, and blankets in New Mexico. Then the caravan traveled more than a thousand miles south to Mexico City. The trail the caravans used was called the *Camino Real*.

When Abuelito got to Mexico City, he traded
the goods he'd brought from New Mexico for things
from all over the world. He traded
for silk and cotton goods and lace,
for iron tools, paper, ink, books,
fine dishes, coffee, and sugar.
Then the caravan would load up
and start the long trip back to New Mexico.

Abuelito had been gone more than six months.
Josefina and her sisters were excited because they
expected Abuelito's caravan to return any day now.
Their rancho was always the caravan's last stop
before the town of Santa Fe, where Abuelito lived.

"I can't wait until Abuelito comes!" said
Josefina. She thought that the arrival of the caravan
was the most exciting thing that happened on the
rancho. The wagons were full of treasures to be
traded in Santa Fe. But the most important treasure
the caravan brought was Abuelito himself, safe and
sound and full of wonderful stories. Sometimes the
caravan went through sandstorms that were so bad
they blocked out the sun. Sometimes robbers or
wild animals attacked the caravan. Sometimes the
caravan had to cross flooded rivers or waterless

deserts. Abuelito loved to tell about his adventures, and the sisters loved to listen.

"I am going to go on the caravan with Abuelito someday," said Francisca, dreamily swirling a shirt in the stream. "I'll see everything there is to see, and then I'll settle down and live in Mexico City with Mamá's sister, our Tía Dolores. I am sure she lives in a grand house and knows all the most elegant people."

Clara rolled her eyes and scrubbed hard with her soap. "That's ridiculous," she said. "We hardly know Tía Dolores. We haven't seen her for the whole ten years she's been living in Mexico City."

Francisca smiled a superior smile. "I am older than you are, Clara," she said. "I was nearly six when Tía Dolores left. I remember her."

"Well," said Clara tartly. "If *she* remembers *you,* I am sure she won't want you to live with her!"

Francisca made a face and was about to say something sharp when Josefina piped up.

"Ana," said Josefina, trying to keep the peace. "What do you hope Abuelito will bring on the caravan?"

"Shoes for my two little boys," Ana answered.

"I hope he brings that plow Papá needs," said Clara. She was always practical.

"How dull!" said Francisca. *"I'm* hoping for some new lace."

"You think too much of how you look," said Clara.

Francisca smirked. "Perhaps you ought—" she began.

But Josefina interrupted again. "Well, I know one thing we *all* hope Abuelito will bring," she said cheerfully. "Chocolate!"

"Lots!" said Francisca and Clara. They spoke at exactly the same moment, which made them laugh at each other.

"You haven't said what you're wishing for," Ana said to Josefina. She was squeezing water out of a petticoat. "Perhaps you're hoping for a surprise."

"Perhaps," said Josefina, smiling.

The truth was, she didn't know how to name what she wished for. What she wanted most was for her sisters to be at peace with one another. She wanted the household to be running smoothly, and Papá to be happy and laughing again. She longed for life to be the way it was when Mamá was alive.

Right after Mamá died, Josefina had felt that the world should end. How could life go on for the rest of them without Mamá? It had seemed wrong, even cruel somehow, that nothing stopped. The sun rose and set. Seasons passed from one to another. There were still chores to be done every day. There were clothes to be washed, weeds to pull, animals to be fed, socks to be mended.

But as the year passed, Josefina began to see that the steady rhythm of life on the rancho was her best comfort. Mamá seemed close by when Josefina and her sisters were together doing the laundry or mending or cooking or cleaning. The sisters tried hard to do the chores the way that Mamá had taught them. Every day, they tried to remember their prayers and their manners and how to do things right. But it was not easy without Mamá's loving guidance.

Josefina looked at the primroses in her pouch and thought of Mamá. Mamá had such faith in them all! She brought out the best in them. Now that she was gone, they struggled. Francisca and Clara squabbled. Ana worried. Josefina often felt lost and unsure. And Papá was very quiet. Josefina sighed. She didn't see how the caravan could bring anything to help them.

"Here comes a surprise," said Clara. "But not one you will like, Josefina."

Josefina looked up. "Oh, no," she said.

It was a small herd of goats. They were coming down the hill to drink from the stream. Josefina disliked all goats and one goat in particular. The biggest, oldest, meanest goat was named Florecita. Florecita was a sneaky, nasty bully. She bit, she rammed, and she'd eat anything. Josefina was afraid of her. She frowned when she spotted Florecita at the edge of the herd.

"Now, Josefina," said Ana when she saw her frowning. "You mustn't dislike *these* goats. This is *our* herd."

Most of the rancho's sheep and goats were still in the summer pastures up in the mountains. But this herd was kept close to the rancho to provide milk to drink and to make into cheese. It was a small herd that had belonged to Mamá. She left the herd to Josefina and her sisters when she died. Josefina wished she hadn't. Mamá had always protected Josefina from things she feared and disliked, and

Mamá had protected Josefina from the goats. "The goats are everything you are not, Josefina," Mamá used to say. "They are bold and loud and disagreeable and mean. It's no wonder you dislike them!" Josefina was sure that Mamá never intended her to have anything to do with the goats, so she avoided them as much as possible.

But right now, Josefina saw Florecita headed straight for her.

"She wants the flowers in your pouch!" warned Francisca.

Josefina put one hand over the flowers. She did not want Florecita to have them. They might be the last primroses of the year!

"Shoo!" she said to Florecita feebly, waving her free hand. "Go away!"

"Shoo! Shoo! Shoo!" cried her sisters with more force.

Florecita didn't even slow down. She kept walking steadily toward Josefina. Her yellow eyes were fixed on the primroses in Josefina's pouch.

"Wave a stick at her," suggested Francisca.

"Splash her," suggested Ana.

"Throw a pebble at her," suggested Clara.

16

But Josefina backed away. She had been poked
by Florecita's sharp horns before, and she had no
wish to be poked again. She scrambled up and stood
on the log over the stream. Still Florecita did not
stop coming. Josefina took one backward step, then
another, then *SPLASH!* She missed her footing and
fell off the log into the stream. It was very shallow,
so she landed hard on the bottom.

"Oh, no!" she wailed. She saw that all but one
sprig of the primroses had fallen out of her pouch.
The flowers were floating on the water. Florecita
snatched them up in her mean-looking teeth. She

chewed them, looking satisfied. Then the goat
turned and sauntered off to rejoin the herd.

"Are you all right?" Ana asked kindly. She
helped Josefina to her feet. "You really must not
let Florecita bully you like that!"

Josefina wrung out her skirt and smiled.
"I tried to stand up to Florecita," she joked, "but
I ended up sitting down, didn't I?"

She laughed along with her sisters, but she
was annoyed with Florecita. She was even more
annoyed with herself for letting Florecita scare her.
As she looked at the one sprig of primroses left in
her pouch, she thought of another thing she wanted
that the caravan could not possibly bring her—the
courage to stand up to Florecita!

CHAPTER
TWO

—

ABUELITO'S
SURPRISE

The afternoon sun was so strong it made the ground shimmer. Josefina dipped the drinking gourd into the water jar and took a long drink. Like everyone else on the rancho, she was up earlier than usual after her *siesta*, the mid-day rest. Papá had heard that the caravan was not far away. It would come this afternoon! Everyone was eagerly bustling about, preparing for its arrival.

Josefina poured some water into her cupped hand and held it to her face, cooling first one cheek and then the other. Then she opened her hand and let the water fall on a small cluster of flowers below. Mamá had planted these flowers, which grew in a protected corner of the back courtyard. Josefina's house was built around two square courtyards. The front courtyard was surrounded by rooms where Josefina and her family lived. The back courtyard was surrounded by workrooms, storerooms, and rooms for the servants. The two courtyards were connected by a narrow passageway.

Mamá, with Josefina at her side, had tended her flowers in the back courtyard with great devotion. She started them from seeds sent to her from Mexico City by her sister, Tía Dolores. Josefina remembered how pleased Mamá had always been when the caravan brought her some seeds from Tía Dolores. It had always seemed like a miracle to Josefina that the small brown seeds could, with water and Mamá's care, grow into beautiful, colorful flowers. Since Mamá died, Josefina had cared for the flowers by herself as best she could. Just now she sprinkled the rest of the water in the drinking gourd on them.

"I'm glad you remember to water your mamá's flowers, Josefina." Josefina turned and saw Papá. He was so tall, she had to lift her chin to look at

his face. "Things grew well for your mamá, didn't they?" Papá added.

"Yes, Papá," Josefina answered. "Mamá loved her flowers."

"So she did," said Papá, dipping the drinking gourd into the water jar. "And I hear Florecita likes flowers, too."

Josefina blushed.

"Don't worry," said Papá. "You'll stand up to Florecita when you're ready."

Josefina grinned a little bashfully. She watched Papá drink his water. Papá's eyebrows were so thick,

he looked fierce until you saw the kindness in his
eyes. All the sisters were respectful and rather shy
of Papá. He had always been saving of his words,
but since Mamá died he'd become especially quiet.
Josefina knew his silence didn't come from sternness
or anger. It came from sadness. She knew because
she often felt the same way.

Mamá used to say that Josefina and Papá were
alike. They were both quiet, except with their family,
but full of ideas inside! Papá didn't have Mamá's
easy manner with people. It had always been Mamá
who remembered the names of everyone in the
village, from the oldest person to the newest baby.
She remembered to ask if an illness was better, or
how the chickens were laying. She gave advice on
everything from growing squash to dyeing wool.
Mamá was well loved and well respected. She was
Papá's partner. She ran the household while he ran
the rancho. Josefina knew that Papá missed Mamá
with all his heart.

Papá tipped the gourd so that the last drops
of water fell on the flowers. He smiled at Josefina,
and then strode off out the gate toward the fields.

Josefina carried the water jar to the kitchen.

"Oh, there you are, Josefina," said Ana. Her hands were covered with flour, so she had to use the back of her wrist to brush the sweat off her forehead. The heat of the cooking fires was making her face red and her hair stick out. Pots full of delicious-smelling concoctions sizzled, steamed, and burbled over the fires.

There was always a big *fandango* in the evening after the caravan arrived. Neighbors from the village, friends from the Indian *pueblo,* and all the people traveling with the caravan were invited. They came to Josefina's family's house to eat and drink and sing and dance and celebrate the caravan's safe return. Mamá had always known just what to do to prepare for the fandango. But this was the first time Ana was in charge. Josefina could see that Ana was overwhelmed even though Carmen, the cook, was helping her. Two other servants were making *tortillas* as quickly as they could. Francisca and Clara were helping, too. They were peeling, chopping, and stirring as fast as their hands could move.

cooking tortillas

"Thank you for the water," said Ana. She

*"Thank you for the water," said Ana. "Now please go to the
kitchen garden and get me some onions."*

handed Josefina a large basket. "Now please go to the kitchen garden and get me some onions."

"I'll come, too," Francisca said. "We need tomatoes."

The kitchen garden was just outside the back courtyard. Josefina always thought the garden looked like a blanket spread on the ground. The neat rows of fruits and vegetables and herbs made colorful stripes. The squash made a yellow stripe. The chiles made a red stripe. The pumpkins were orange, the melons were light green, and the beans were dark green. In between the rows, the earth was a dark reddish-brown, thanks to the water the girls carried up from the stream every day. A stick fence like a blanket's fringe surrounded the garden to keep hungry animals out. The sisters were all proud of the garden.

Josefina had gathered a basketful of onions when suddenly she stood up. Francisca stood up, too, and the girls looked at each other.

"Is it . . . ?" Francisca began.

"Shhh . . ." said Josefina, holding her finger to her lips. She tilted her head and listened hard.

Yes! There it was. She could hear the rumble and squeak of wooden wheels that meant only one thing. The caravan was coming!

Francisca heard, too. The girls smiled at each other, grabbed their baskets, and ran as fast as they could back through the gate. "The caravan! It's coming!" they shouted. "Ana! Clara! It's coming!" They dropped their baskets outside the kitchen door as Clara rushed out to join them.

The three girls dashed across the front courtyard and flew up the steps of the tower in the south wall. The window in the tower was narrow, so Josefina knelt and looked out the lower part. Francisca and Clara stood behind her and looked over her head.

At first, all they saw was a cloud of dust stirring on the road from the village. Then the sound of the wheels grew louder and louder. Soon they heard the jingle of harnesses, dogs barking, people shouting, and the village church bell ringing. Next they saw soldiers coming over the hill with the sun glinting on their buttons and guns. Then came mule after mule. It looked

like a hundred or more to Josefina. The mules were
carrying heavy packs strapped to their backs. She
counted thirty carts pulled by plodding oxen. The
carts lumbered along on their two big wooden
wheels. There were four-wheeled wagons
as well. And so many people! Too many
to count! There were muleteers, cart
drivers, traders, and whole families of
travelers. There were herders driving
sheep, goats, and cattle. Villagers, and

muleteer

Indians from the nearby pueblo, walked along
with the caravan to welcome it.

Francisca stood on tiptoe to see better. She put
her hands on Josefina's shoulders. "Don't you love
to think about all the places the caravan has been?"
she asked. "And all the places the things it brings
come from, too?"

"Yes," said Josefina. "They come from all over
the world, up the Camino Real, right to *our* door!"

Most of the caravan stopped and set up camp
midway between the village and the rancho. But
many muleteers and some of the cart drivers
camped closer to the house, in a shady area next
to the stream. Josefina saw Papá ride his horse up

to one of the big, four-wheeled wagons. He waved to its driver.

"That's Abuelito!" Josefina cried. She pointed to the driver of the four-wheeled wagon. "Look! Papá is greeting him. See? There he is!"

Francisca leaned forward. "Who's that tall woman sitting next to Abuelito?" she wondered aloud. "She's greeting Papá as if she knows him."

But Josefina and Clara had already turned away from the window. They hurried down from the tower. Josefina ran to the kitchen and stuck her head in the door. "Come on," she said to Ana. "Papá and Abuelito are on their way up to the house."

"Oh dear, oh dear," fussed Ana as she wiped her hands and smoothed her hair. "There's still so much to do. I'll never be ready for the fandango."

When Papá led Abuelito's big wagon up to the front gate, Josefina was the first to run out and greet it. Francisca, Clara, and Ana were close behind. Josefina thought she'd never seen a sight as wonderful as Abuelito's happy face. He handed the reins to the woman next to him and climbed down.

"My beautiful granddaughters!" said Abuelito. He kissed them as he named them. "Ana, and

Francisca! Clara, and my little Josefina! Oh,
God bless you! God bless you! It is good to see
you! This was the finest trip I've ever made! Oh,
the adventures, the adventures! But I am getting
too old for these trips. They make me old before
my time. This is my last trip. My last."

"Oh, Abuelito!" said Francisca, taking his arm
and laughing. "You say that every time!"

Abuelito threw back his head and laughed, too.
"Ah, but this time I mean it," he said. "I've brought
a surprise for you." He turned and held out his hand
to the tall woman on the wagon. "Here she is, your
Tía Dolores. She has come back to live with her
mamá and me in Santa Fe. Now I have no reason
to go to Mexico City ever again!"

Josefina and her sisters looked so surprised,
Papá and Abuelito laughed at them. Tía Dolores
took Abuelito's hand and gracefully swung herself
down from the wagon seat.

Papá smiled at her. "You see, Dolores? You have
surprised my daughters as much as you surprised
me," he said. "Welcome to our home."

"Gracias," Tía Dolores answered. She smiled at
Papá and then she turned to the sisters. "I've looked

forward to this moment for a long time!" she said
to them. "I've wanted to see all of you! My dear
sister's children!"

She spoke to each one in turn. "You're very
like your mamá, Ana," she said. "And Francisca,
you've grown so tall and so beautiful! Dear Clara,
you were barely three years old when I left. Do you
remember?"

Tía Dolores took Josefina's hand in both of her
own. She bent forward so that she could look closely
at Josefina's face. "At last I meet you, Josefina," she
said. "You weren't even born when I left. And look!
Here you are! Already a lovely young girl!" Tía
Dolores straightened again. Her eyes were bright
as she looked at all the sisters. "I'm so happy to
see you all. It's good to be back."

The girls were still too surprised to say much,
but they smiled shyly at Tía Dolores. Ana was
the first to collect herself. "Please, Abuelito and
Tía Dolores. Come inside and have a cool drink. I'm
sure you're tired and thirsty." She led Tía Dolores
inside the gate. "You must excuse us, Tía Dolores,"
she said. "We haven't prepared any place for you
to sleep."

"I've looked forward to this moment for a long time!" Tía Dolores said.
"I've wanted to see all of you! My dear sister's children!"

"Goodness, Ana!" said Tía Dolores. "You didn't know I was coming. I didn't know myself, really, until the last minute. I've been caring for my dear aunt in Mexico City all these years. Bless her soul! She died this past spring. It was just before Abuelito's caravan arrived. I had no reason to stay. So, I joined the caravan to come home."

"Yes," Abuelito said to the girls. "Your grandmother will be so pleased! Wait till Dolores and I get to Santa Fe the day after tomorrow! What a surprise, eh?"

Josefina could not take her eyes off Tía Dolores as everyone sat down together in the family *sala*. The room's thick walls and small windows kept it cool even in the heat of the afternoon.

Francisca whispered, "Isn't Tía Dolores's dress beautiful? Her sleeves must be the latest style from Europe."

But Josefina hadn't noticed Tía Dolores's sleeves, or anything else about her clothes. *This is Tía Dolores,* she kept thinking. *This is Mamá's sister.*

Josefina studied Tía Dolores to see if she looked like Mamá. Mamá had been the older of the two sisters, but Tía Dolores was much taller. She didn't have Mamá's soft, rounded beauty, Josefina decided, nor her pale skin or dark, smooth hair. Everything about Tía Dolores was sharper somehow. Her hands were bigger. Her face was more narrow. She had gray eyes and dark red hair that was springy. Her voice didn't sound like Mamá's, either. Mamá's voice was high and breathy, like notes from a flute. Tía Dolores's voice had a graceful sound. It was as low and clear as notes from a harp string. But when Tía Dolores laughed, Josefina was startled. Her laugh sounded so much like Mamá's! If Josefina closed her eyes, it might be Mamá laughing.

There was a great deal of laughter in the family sala that afternoon as Abuelito told the story of his trip. Josefina sat next to Abuelito, her arms wrapped around her knees. She was happy. It reminded her of the old days to sit with her family this way and listen to Abuelito tell about his adventures.

"This was the most remarkable trip I've ever had," said Abuelito. "Oh, the trip to Mexico City was dull enough. But on the way home! Bless my soul! What an adventure! We were in terrible danger. Terrible! Terrible! And your Tía Dolores saved us."

"Oh, but I didn't—" Tía Dolores began.

"No, no, no, my dear daughter! You *did* save us," said Abuelito. He turned to Papá and the girls. "You see," he said, "I was so glad that Dolores was going to come home with me. I finished all my business in Mexico City as quickly as I could. All went well until the day I came to Dolores's house to load up her belongings. Then the trouble began." He lowered his voice, pretending he did not want Tía Dolores to hear. "I had forgotten how stubborn your Tía Dolores is. She is perhaps the most stubborn woman in the world. What did she insist that we bring? You'll never guess! Her piano!"

Amazed, the girls all repeated, "Her *piano?*"

"Yes!" said Abuelito. He was pleased to have astonished them all. "Such fuss and trouble! I told her it was too heavy and too big! But she said she'd sooner leave all her other belongings than her piano. So I grumbled, but I allowed the piano to be packed and loaded onto one of my wagons. We left Mexico City, and I complained about the piano every mile of the way." He shook his head. "Your Tía Dolores never said a word. She just let me go on

34

and on, complaining. Well, then we came to Dead
Man's Canyon. And do you know what happened?"

"What?" asked the girls.

"Thieves!" cried Abuelito in a voice so loud
the girls jumped. "Thieves attacked the caravan!
Oh, you've never seen such a fight! Shouting,
swordfights, gunshots! The wagon with the piano
was just behind ours. We saw two thieves climb up
on it and push the driver onto the ground. Then six
or seven of our men rushed over and wrestled with
the two thieves, trying to pull them off the wagon.
With all the yelling and fighting, the oxen harnessed
to that wagon were scared. They bumbled into each
other trying to get away. The wagon lurched
forward, right to the edge of a deep
gully. And then *crash!* Over it fell!
Into the gully!"

The girls gasped.

Abuelito put his hand on his heart.
"God bless us and save us all! What a sound that
piano made when it fell!" he said. "A thud, and
then a hollow *BOOM* that rumbled like musical
thunder! It sounded like a giant had strummed all
the keys in one stroke. The terrible sound bounced

off the walls of Dead Man's Canyon. It seemed to grow louder with every echo. The thieves were terrified! They'd never heard such a sound in all their lives. Well! Didn't they take off as if they were on fire? All of them ran away as fast as their thieving legs could carry them! I'll bet they are still running!"

Everyone laughed. Abuelito laughed most of all, remembering with pleasure how frightened the thieves were. When he stopped laughing he said, "After that, I put the piano in my own wagon. I never complained again. And so you see! Dolores did save us all, by insisting that we bring her piano."

"Well done, Dolores!" said Papá.

"But Abuelito," said Josefina. "Was the piano badly hurt?"

Tía Dolores answered. "No, child," she said. "One leg is splintered, and the top is scratched. But I think it will sound fine."

"Oh," Josefina blurted, "may we see it?"

"No, no, no," said Abuelito. "We had to rebuild the crate. It's too much trouble to open it up. You'll just have to come to Santa Fe sometime to hear your aunt play."

Papá cleared his throat. "The girls and I have never seen or heard a piano," he said. "May I open the crate? I'll close it up afterward."

Tía Dolores turned to Abuelito. "Please," she said. "I'd like the girls to hear the piano."

Abuelito laughed and shrugged. "Of course, my dear, of course!" he said. "How can I say no to you after you saved my caravan?"

Tía Dolores kissed him. Then she and Papá led the girls outside to the wagon. The piano was in a big wooden crate. Papá pried a few boards off the crate. Tía Dolores climbed into the wagon. She reached into the crate and pushed back the lid that protected the piano's keys. She couldn't stand up straight, and she didn't have much room to move her hands, but she played a chord. And then, as Papá and the four girls listened, she played a spirited tune.

Josefina felt the music thrum through her whole body. It made her shiver with delight. The notes were muffled because the piano was in the wooden crate, but to Josefina, the notes sounded as beautiful as bells all chiming together in harmony.

She had never heard music like the piano's music before. The notes were so full, so perfect and delicate, that Josefina imagined she could almost *see* them as they filled the air.

Josefina listened. She realized that, through the music, Tía Dolores was telling them how happy she was. The music expressed her happiness better than words ever could, because it made all of them hearing it happy, too. Josefina stood still, barely breathing, listening hard until Tía Dolores stopped.

"Oh, dear," said Tía Dolores. "I'm afraid the piano's a little out of tune and I'm a little out of practice." Gently, she closed the lid over the keys.

Josefina wanted very much to touch the piano keys. She wanted to make the wonderful music happen herself. But she was too shy to ask Tía Dolores, so she said nothing.

"Gracias, Dolores," said Papá as he helped her climb down from the wagon.

"Oh, yes, gracias," said Ana, Francisca, and Clara.

"You must all come to see me in Santa Fe," said Tía Dolores, smiling. "I'll play for you, and show you how to play the piano yourselves."

The three oldest sisters followed Tía Dolores back inside the house. But Josefina stood next to the wagon until Papá had finished closing the crate. She wanted to stay near the piano as long as she could. She knew she would never forget the way Tía Dolores's music had sounded, or the way it had made her feel.

When Papá was finished, he saw Josefina. "You liked the piano music, didn't you?" he asked.

"Oh, yes, Papá," answered Josefina. "I didn't want Tía Dolores to stop."

Papá smiled. "I didn't either," he said. "Well, there will be plenty of fiddle music at the fandango tonight. You'd better go in now and get ready. The guests will be coming soon."

"Yes, Papá," Josefina answered. She took one last look at the piano crate, then started back inside. As she walked, she thought, *I wish there were some way I could let Tía Dolores know how much I loved the piano music. I wish I could give her something in return. But what?*

Later, when Josefina walked into the back courtyard, she knew the answer to her question. She thought of a fine gift to give Tía Dolores.

I'll give it to her during the fandango tonight, she decided. She was pleased with her idea. She thought Tía Dolores would be pleased, too.

C H A P T E R

T H R E E

A GIFT FOR
TÍA DOLORES

brush and ribbon

"Stand still, Josefina," said Francisca. She was slowly and carefully brushing Josefina's hair with a brush made of stiff grasses. Abuelito had brought all four sisters beautiful blue silk hair ribbons. Francisca had put herself in charge of tying them for Josefina and Clara. Josefina fidgeted. She was grateful to Francisca, but she wished she'd *hurry up*. Josefina wanted to be ready for the fandango early, so that she could prepare her gift for Tía Dolores.

Clara tied her sash neatly, then undid it and tied it all over again. Francisca had already brushed Clara's hair and put the blue hair ribbon in it. "Do you think I look all right?" Clara asked.

Josefina and Francisca were surprised. It wasn't
like Clara to worry about her appearance. Josefina
was afraid Francisca might say something unkind.
She was glad when Francisca looked at Clara for
a moment and then said seriously, "You look very
pretty. The blue suits you."

Clara beamed. She reached up to touch her hair
ribbon.

It made Josefina happy to see her sisters getting
along. *It's because Tía Dolores is here,* she thought.
Francisca and Clara were in complete agreement
about Tía Dolores. They both admired her very
much. Josefina smiled to herself. Francisca and
Clara would be pleased when *they* saw her gift for
Tía Dolores, too.

"Finished!" said Francisca. She gave Josefina's
ribbon one last adjustment. "You look fine. Use
your wings and fly away now, Josefina. I can tell
you're anxious to go."

"Gracias, Francisca," Josefina called back over
her shoulder as she hurried from the room.

The sun had set. Cool evening air slid down
from the mountains, bringing darkness with it.
Small bonfires were lit in the front courtyard for

light and for warmth. As she crossed the courtyard,
Josefina could hear Ana and Carmen thanking some
neighbor women who had come early with dishes
of food for the fandango. No one noticed Josefina
slip into the kitchen. She took a small water jar and
slipped out again.

In the back courtyard, Josefina knelt in front
of Mamá's flowers. One by one, she picked all the
freshest and brightest-colored flowers. She put them
in the water jar. Josefina was careful to break the
flowers off near the ground so that the stems were
long, but she didn't disturb the roots. There were
not very many flowers, so Josefina had to pick
almost all of them in order to have a bouquet
anywhere near big enough and beautiful enough
to give to Tía Dolores.

The corner looked bare when she was through.
It's all right, she told herself. *Mamá would approve.
After all, Tía Dolores was the one who sent Mamá the
seeds, so Tía Dolores should be the one to enjoy the
flowers. They* should *be a gift for her.*

Josefina straightened the flowers in the water
jar. The bouquet looked scrawny somehow. So
Josefina slipped the blue ribbon out of her hair and

tied it around the flowers in a
big bow. *There!* she thought with
satisfaction. *That looks much better.*
She wanted the bouquet to be a
surprise for everyone, so she looked
around for a place to hide it. She had
just entered the narrow passageway
between the front and back courtyards when she
bumped into Papá.

"What's this you've got here?" asked Papá,
peering at Josefina over the tops of the flowers.

"It's . . . they're a gift for Tía Dolores,"
explained Josefina. "I wanted to give her something
to thank her for the music."

It was too dark to see Papá's face clearly, but
Josefina could tell by his voice that he was smiling.
"I think that is a very fine idea," he said. "I'll tell
you what. I am going to make a formal introduction
of Tía Dolores to all our friends and neighbors at
the fandango tonight. After I do, perhaps you will
give Tía Dolores the bouquet."

"Yes, I will!" said Josefina happily.

"Very well," said Papá. "It will be our secret
until then."

"Gracias, Papá," said Josefina. After Papá left, Josefina put the jar of flowers under the bench in the passageway. No one would see it there, and she would be able to fetch it quickly when it was time to give it to Tía Dolores.

More guests arrived every moment. They called out a chorus of greetings to each other as they crossed the front courtyard to the *gran sala,* the family's finest room. Because this was a very special night, the gran sala was lit with candles. Their wavering light made the guests' shadows swoop and dance on the walls.

Soon the musicians struck up a lively tune on their fiddles and the real dancing began. It seemed to Josefina that the dancers flew around the room with as much ease as their shadows had. Their feet hardly seemed to touch the floor at all as they whirled by in a blur of bright colors.

No one whirled faster than Francisca. No one looked happier or more beautiful. In the candlelight, her dark curly hair seemed to shine like a black stone in the stream. And Josefina was glad to see that Ana had put her responsibilities aside for a while and was dancing with her husband, Tomás. All around the sides of the gran sala, older ladies sat holding babies on their laps so that the babies' young mothers could dance. The old ladies clapped the babies' hands in time to the music.

Josefina and Clara were still too young to be allowed to dance, so they stood outside in the courtyard and leaned on the windowsill, looking in at the dancers. Josefina's feet danced along to the music. It was impossible to be still! The music seemed to twist and turn in the air, wind its way around all the dancers, and find its way outside to tickle Josefina's feet so that they just had to move.

Every once in a while, over the music and conversation, Josefina and Clara could hear Abuelito's voice. He'd be saying, "Boom! What a sound! Those thieves ran off and I'll bet they're running still." Clara and Josefina grinned at each other. Abuelito was telling the story about Tía Dolores's piano over and over again. The girls noticed that the number of thieves grew larger every time Abuelito told the story!

It seemed to Josefina that the dancers flew around the room with as much ease as their shadows had. They whirled by in a blur of bright colors.

The person both girls liked best to watch was Tía Dolores. She was easy to pick out of the crowd because she was so tall, and because no one else had hair of quite such a rich, dark red.

"She dances well, doesn't she?" said Clara as Tía Dolores swept by.

"Yes," said Josefina. "She's as graceful as . . . as the music."

Soon Papá came by the window and nodded to Josefina. Josefina nodded back.

"What's that all about?" asked Clara.

"It's a surprise," said Josefina, excited and smiling. "Stay here and you'll see."

She scurried across the courtyard to the passageway where she'd left the bouquet. It was very dark. Josefina bent down and felt under the bench for the water jar with the bouquet in it. It wasn't there. *That's odd,* she thought.

Josefina stood up, perplexed. And then she saw the jar. It was lying on its side near one wall. It was empty. *Where is the bouquet?* Josefina wondered anxiously.

She looked all around the passageway. The bouquet was nowhere to be seen, but an odd white shape looming in the back courtyard caught her eye. She walked toward it and gasped. Oh, no! The white shape was Florecita! The goat must have broken out of her pen and found her way into the back courtyard. Josefina did *not* want to put Florecita back in her pen.

When she turned away to get help, she stepped on something. She stooped down and picked it up. At first she didn't know what it was. And then she saw. It was a few green stems held together by a trampled, mud-stained blue ribbon. Suddenly, Josefina realized what had happened. *Florecita had eaten the bouquet!* This was all that was left of the flowers she had picked for Tía Dolores.

But that was not the worst of it. At that instant, Josefina saw what Florecita was doing. Calm as could be, Florecita was standing smack in the middle of what used to be Mamá's flowers. She was chewing a mouthful of stems. One hollyhock, root and all, dangled from her mouth. Josefina could see that no other flowers were left. All that remained were some scraggly, chewed, crushed, and broken stems and a scattering of leaves and petals on the ground.

Florecita turned her nasty yellow eyes on Josefina. The goat looked very satisfied with herself.

Josefina was furious. "Florecita!" she hissed in a ferocious whisper. "You awful, awful animal! You've ruined *everything.*"

Josefina was so angry she forgot to be afraid of Florecita. She marched right up to the goat and yanked the hollyhock out of her mouth. Florecita looked surprised. She looked even more surprised when Josefina swatted her on the back with the stems, saying, "How could you? You ate the bouquet and you killed Mamá's flowers. Oh, I *hate* you, Florecita!"

Josefina shoved Florecita hard. Then she took hold of one of Florecita's fearsome horns and pulled with all her strength. "Come with me," she said. Josefina dragged Florecita to her pen. She slammed the gate shut. "I hate you, Florecita," she said again. "I'll hate you forever!"

Josefina ran all the way back to the bench in the passageway and slumped down on it. There was nothing to be done. She looked at the dirty blue ribbon and the chewed stems wilting in her hand and fought back tears of disappointment.

"Josefina?" a voice said. "What are you doing here in the darkness?"

Josefina looked up. She saw Tía Dolores coming toward her. Josefina could hardly talk. She showed the sad-looking stems to Tía Dolores. "This was a bouquet for you," she said in a shaky voice. "But our goat Florecita found it and ate it. And she killed Mamá's flowers, too."

"Ah," said Tía Dolores. She sat next to Josefina on the bench.

Slowly, Josefina explained. "I wanted to give you a gift to thank you for the piano music," she said. "So I picked all the best flowers. I tied my new hair ribbon around them. The flowers were so pretty. They grew from the seeds you sent Mamá. I've been watering them since Mamá died, because I know she loved them. Now there are none left. There will never be any more. The flowers are dead."

Tía Dolores was a good listener. She sat still and gave Josefina her full attention. Neither one of them noticed the noise and laughter coming from the gran sala. The fandango seemed far away. When Josefina was finished explaining, Tía Dolores said, "Show me your mamá's flowers."

Josefina led Tía Dolores to the corner of
the back courtyard. "You see," she said. "There
is nothing left."

Tía Dolores knelt down. She looked at what
was left of the flowers. She scooped up a handful
of soil and rubbed it between her fingers. Gently,
she touched the short, bitten-off stems.

Then she smiled at Josefina. "Don't worry,"
she said. "Your mamá planted these flowers well.
The roots are deep and strong. You've kept them
healthy by watering the soil. They'll live, I promise."
She stood and brushed the soil off her hands. "Do

you like caring for flowers?" she asked.

Josefina nodded. "I used to help Mamá," she said.

"I brought some seeds with me when I left Mexico City," said Tía Dolores. "Perhaps you and I can plant them tomorrow."

"Oh, could we?" said Josefina.

"Yes," said Tía Dolores. "We'll wash your hair ribbon, too. Now we had better go back to the gran sala."

Papá met them at the door. "Josefina," he said. "Where have you been? I introduced Tía Dolores, but then I couldn't find you."

"Oh, Papá," said Josefina. "Florecita ate the bouquet! And then she almost ruined all the rest of Mamá's flowers."

"Ah, that's too bad," said Papá sadly. He looked around the courtyard. "Is Florecita loose?"

"No," said Josefina. "I dragged her back to her pen and shut the gate."

"You did?" asked Papá. "But I thought you were afraid of Florecita."

"I am," said Josefina. "I mean, I *was*. I guess just now I was so angry at Florecita I forgot!"

Papá laughed. "Well, we never know where our courage is going to come from!" he said. "I am sorry about the flowers, though."

"Tía Dolores says the flowers will be all right," said Josefina. "She's going to help me plant new seeds tomorrow."

"Is she?" said Papá. He turned and smiled at Tía Dolores. "Well, then, Dolores," he said, "that means you'll have to come back often. You'll have to visit us to see how the flowers are coming along."

"I will," said Tía Dolores. "God willing."

"Come inside and have something to eat now," said Papá. "Ana would never forgive us if we didn't enjoy the food she's prepared."

Josefina followed Papá and Tía Dolores into the gran sala. She grinned to herself. *I guess the caravan didn't need to bring me the courage to stand up to Florecita after all,* she thought. *It turns out I already had it. But I might never have found out if I hadn't picked a bouquet for Tía Dolores.*

An idea danced through Josefina's head just then. As quick as the flicker of starlight on water, the idea appeared and disappeared. But it was an

idea that would come again and again all the rest
of the night and through the next day, until it grew
from an idea into a heartfelt hope.

CHAPTER
FOUR

JOSEFINA'S IDEA

sheepskins

Never had Josefina been more eager to begin a day. The next morning she was up even earlier than usual. Quietly, so that she wouldn't waken Francisca or Clara, Josefina rolled up the sheepskins and blankets that were her bed. She dressed and slipped outside. The moon hung low in the sky. It cast such a strong, pure light that everything was bathed in silver or shadow.

Josefina went to the kitchen. Early as it was, Carmen was already there grinding corn for the morning meal. Her husband was starting the kitchen fire. Carmen nodded good morning to Josefina and handed her a water jar to fill at the stream, just as she did every morning. But this morning was different for Josefina. This was the morning of the day Tía Dolores was going to spend with her and her sisters.

The huge front gate was closed, so Josefina stepped through the small door cut into the gate. She closed the door behind her and ran across the moon-washed ground to Abuelito's wagon. Standing on tiptoe, she looked in. There was the big crate with Tía Dolores's piano inside. Josefina poked her finger through a crack in the crate and touched the polished wood of the piano. She smiled when she remembered the pleasure its music had given her. Then she skipped down to the stream, thinking of the melody Tía Dolores had played.

The tune stayed in her head as she did her early-morning chores. She gathered eggs singing it. She swept the courtyards dancing to it. She piled wood next to the fireplaces in time to its rhythm. When the village church bell rang its call to prayers at seven o'clock, it seemed to ring along with the tune. And when the family said morning prayers together in front of the small altar in the family sala, dedicating their day's work to God, their voices seemed to rise and fall just as the piano notes had.

The music seemed to be everywhere Josefina went. Tía Dolores did, too! Tía Dolores was interested in everything. At breakfast she said, "I want to see as much of the rancho as I can today."

So after breakfast Josefina led Tía Dolores through the orchard, past the cornfields, and to the stream. They filled water jars and carried them up to water the kitchen garden. Then they picked some fat pumpkins for Tía Dolores to take home with her to Santa Fe the next day. "I am sure my mother has no pumpkins as big as these in her garden!" said Tía Dolores.

Wherever she went, Tía Dolores found something to praise. Josefina led Tía Dolores to the weaving room. There Clara showed her the sheep's wool she had carded, spun, and dyed. Tía Dolores admired the colors. "There are no colors finer than these in all of Mexico," she said.

Clara's wool

Tía Dolores was a good teacher. She showed Clara a faster way to knit the heel on a sock. She showed Francisca how to sew a patch over a hole so that it hardly showed at all.

Josefina was in the back courtyard clearing away the dead stems Florecita had trampled when Tía Dolores joined her.

"I've brought you some seeds to plant," she said to Josefina as she handed her a small package.

"Gracias!" said Josefina.

"I'll help you for a while. Then I promised Ana I would make bread with her," said Tía Dolores. She began to dig holes in the soil for the seeds. "Ana has lots of responsibilities, doesn't she?"

"Yes," agreed Josefina. "It's hard for Ana. Mamá ran the household so smoothly. But Ana doesn't always know what to do, and Mamá is not here to teach her."

"Ana is young," said Tía Dolores as she covered some seeds with soil. "It's a good thing she has you and Francisca and Clara to help her."

Josefina nodded slowly. "We try," she said. "But sometimes . . ." She stopped.

Tía Dolores gave her a questioning look.

Josefina sighed. She dug a little hole in the soil. "You see," she said, "Francisca and Clara fight a lot. They are so different! Clara is careful and practical, and Francisca is so quick and fiery. When Mamá was alive, she put a stop to their arguments before they began. But now . . . Well, Ana tries, but she is too soft-hearted and they won't mind her. I try to joke them out of fighting. Sometimes it works. But sometimes it doesn't."

"'Blessed are the peacemakers,'" said Tía Dolores softly, "'for they will be called the children of God.'" She smiled at Josefina. "You know," she said, "it's perfectly natural for sisters to disagree. You should have heard your mamá and me sometimes! She was quite a few years older than I was. I am sure she thought I was a miserable pest. I wanted to be like her. Once I wore her best sash without her permission, and I lost it. Your mamá was very angry. She wouldn't speak to me for days. But she finally forgave me."

Josefina realized suddenly, *Tía Dolores misses her sister. She misses Mamá, too, just as much as we do.* She said, "I wish you could be here to protect these flowers from Florecita when they bloom."

"I'd love to see the flowers," said Tía Dolores. "But *you* can protect them from Florecita. You aren't afraid of her anymore. You don't need me. You will make your mamá's flowers bloom again and keep them safe, Josefina. I know you will."

"Oh, Tía Dolores! It's beautiful!" said Ana. She draped a silk rebozo over her shoulders. Its colors were as bright as flowers. "Gracias!"

It was early afternoon, just after the mid-day meal. Ana, Francisca, Clara, and Josefina were gathered in the family sala. Tía Dolores had called them together. She had presents for them all.

"Francisca," said Tía Dolores. "This is a sewing diary I made for you." She gave Francisca a little handmade book. "There are sketches of dresses in it, and samples of material, and notes about how to make the dresses."

"Gracias!" said Francisca. Eagerly, she looked at the sewing diary. "The dresses are so elegant, Tía Dolores!" she said. "I wish you could be here to help us make them." She looked up and joked, "I'm afraid I will sew a sleeve on upside down!"

"The notes and directions will help you," said Tía Dolores.

Francisca looked doubtful. "But I can't read," she said. "None of us can."

"Oh!" said Tía Dolores. "Well, then! Just use your good sense. I am sure if you and your sisters help each other, you will do very well."

For Clara, Tía Dolores had brought a fine pair of scissors and some sewing needles. Clara was very pleased, because her gift was beautiful *and* useful.

"And this is for you, Josefina," said Tía Dolores. She handed Josefina a necklace. A small, dark red stone surrounded by gold hung from a delicate chain.

Josefina smiled. The necklace was lovely. "Gracias, Tía Dolores," she said. Her hands were shaky with excitement as she put the necklace on.

"My!" said Francisca. "Isn't that necklace quite grown-up?"

"Yes, indeed it is," said Tía Dolores firmly. "And isn't Josefina quite grown-up, too?"

Francisca said no more.

"Tía Dolores," said Ana. "How did you know what would be the perfect gift for each one of us?"

Tía Dolores smiled. "All the years I lived in

"Gracias, Tía Dolores," Josefina said. Her hands were shaky with
excitement as she put the necklace on.

Mexico City, I looked forward to the caravans coming," she said. "I knew Abuelito would bring stories about all of you and your life here on the rancho. Sometimes he would bring a letter dictated by your mamá. I felt as if I were watching you grow up even though I was far away. When I decided to come home, I enjoyed thinking about what present to bring each of you."

"Well," said Ana. "I'm sorry we didn't know that you were coming. We have nothing to give you in return for your gifts."

"Oh," laughed Tía Dolores. "This day with you is all the gift I want."

When the afternoon had cooled into early evening, Tía Dolores and Abuelito walked to the village. They wanted to say a prayer at Mamá's grave. They were also going to visit Papá's oldest sister, who lived in the village.

Josefina and her sisters sat in a corner of the front courtyard that was still warm from the heat of the day's sun. Every now and then they could hear Ana's little boys laughing with Carmen in the kitchen nearby. The sisters were peeling back the husks from roasted ears of corn. They were going to braid the husks together to make a long string of ears so that the corn could be hung out to dry.

Josefina said, "Hasn't it been nice today, having Tía Dolores here?"

"Yes!" said Ana. "She was such a help to me! And she was so kind to my little boys."

"Tía Dolores is a very sensible, hardworking person," said Clara. That was her highest praise.

"Oh, Clara!" protested Francisca. "You make her sound as dull as these ears of corn! I found her to be elegant and graceful."

Josefina decided the time had come to tell her sisters her idea. She picked up an ear of corn and peeled the husk slowly. "What if," she said quietly, "we asked Tía Dolores to stay?"

No one said anything. They were all too surprised.

Josefina went on. "She could help us and teach us, the way she did today."

"She wouldn't stay," said Francisca. "She's used to life in Mexico City, where there are lots of grand people and grand houses. She doesn't want to live on a rancho."

"But she said she always loved to hear

Josefina picked up an ear of corn and peeled the husk slowly.
"What if," she said quietly, "we asked Tía Dolores to stay?"

about the rancho when Abuelito came to visit her, remember?" said Josefina. "And she doesn't act fancy or put on airs. She likes it here. She was interested in everything."

"Yes," said Ana. "But I think perhaps she has come home hoping to get married and start a family of her own. She's not too old for that, you know."

"She wouldn't have to stay here forever," said Josefina. "Just for a few months. And anyway, she is our aunt. We *are* her family."

Clara picked up several ears of corn and put them in her lap. "Well," she said in her flat, no-nonsense manner. "Even if Tía Dolores would be willing to stay, it wouldn't be proper for *us* to ask her. Papá would have to approve of the idea. He would have to be the one to ask her to stay."

Josefina's heart sank. She hadn't thought of that. She knew Clara was right.

"Who wants to be the one to present the idea to Papá?" Clara asked. "I certainly don't." She turned to Josefina. "It's your idea," she said. "Do you want to talk to Papá about it?"

Josefina looked down at the ear of corn in her hands. "No," she said in a small voice.

"Will you go to him, Ana?" Clara asked. "You are the oldest."

"Oh, I couldn't!" said Ana. "Papá might think I was complaining. If I say that I need Tía Dolores's help, he might think I don't want to do what it is my responsibility to do."

"Oh!" exclaimed Francisca. She stood up and brushed off her skirt. *"I'm* not afraid to talk to Papá. I'll just march right up to him and say, 'Papá! You must ask Tía Dolores to stay!'"

Ana, Clara, and Josefina looked at each other. They knew that was not at all the right way to speak to Papá! It wasn't that Papá was stern or cold. But he was the *patrón,* the head of the rancho and the head of their family. The girls had never presented such an important idea to him before. It would have to be done politely and with respect.

"Wait, Francisca!" said Josefina. She stood up, too. "I think all of us should speak to Papá. We should go together. That way Papá will see that all four of us would like Tía Dolores to stay."

Ana and Clara didn't move.

"Come on," said Josefina. She grinned. "Don't worry. I'll do the talking if you don't want to. Last night I had the courage to stand up to Florecita. Papá is much, much kinder than *she* is!"

The sisters found Papá near the animal pens. He was tightening the latch on the gate.

He smiled when he saw Josefina. "The latch is stronger now," he said. "We shouldn't have any more goats in Mamá's flowers."

"That's good!" said Josefina. She swallowed. Francisca gave her a little shove forward. "Papá," Josefina said. "May we ask you something?"

Papá looked at the four girls. "Yes?" he said.

"Do you think," Josefina said carefully, "that you could ask Tía Dolores to stay here with us for a while?"

"Ask her to stay?" repeated Papá.

"Yes," said Josefina. "Not forever, just for a while. She could help us. And she could teach us, the way . . . the way Mamá did. Please, would you ask her?"

Josefina saw a look of sadness cross Papá's face. He turned away. "I'll consider it," he said.

"But Papá," Francisca blurted. "You must—"

Josefina tugged on Francisca's sleeve and frowned at her to make her stop talking.

"Gracias, Papá," said Josefina. She hesitated, and then she added, "We need Tía Dolores."

Then she and her sisters left.

❋

"What do you think Papá will do?" Francisca whispered. She and Clara and Josefina were in their sleeping sala, getting ready for bed. "Do you think he will speak to Tía Dolores?"

"I don't know," said Josefina. "I hope so."

"And if he does ask her, what do you think she will say?" Francisca wondered aloud.

Josefina sighed. "I don't know," she said again.

"I think you're silly to wonder about it," Clara said. "We'll find out tomorrow. Abuelito and the caravan will leave first thing in the morning. Tía Dolores will either leave with him or not. We'll just have to wait and see."

"Oh! I hate waiting!" said Francisca.

The three sisters smiled at each other. They all hated to wait! On that they certainly agreed!

The next morning, they were up early. Even Francisca, who was usually slow getting dressed, was ready and waiting with Ana, Clara, and Josefina

next to Abuelito's wagon. They
watched the servants load Abuelito's
small trunk onto the wagon.

Then, with sinking hearts, the sisters saw
Tía Dolores's trunk loaded onto the wagon as well.

"Papá didn't ask her!" Francisca groaned.

"Or maybe he did, and she said no," said Ana.

"She doesn't want to stay," Clara added.

Josefina was so disappointed she couldn't talk.
A lump rose in her throat when she heard Papá and
Tía Dolores and Abuelito coming. Suddenly, Josefina
didn't want to stand there by the wagon one second
longer. She couldn't bear to kiss Tía Dolores and
Abuelito good-bye.

Without a murmur, she slipped away, back
inside the house. She went to the gran sala because
it was the only room that was sure to be empty. As
she walked into the cool darkness of the gran sala,
she remembered how it had looked the night of the
fandango, full of life and music. Now there was
nothing but shadows.

Just then, in a corner of the room, Josefina
saw a large, dark shape. She caught her breath
when she saw what it was.

It was Tía Dolores's piano.
Instantly, Josefina knew what that
meant. Tía Dolores would never
have left her piano, unless . . .

Josefina flew across the courtyard and out the
front gate so fast it seemed as if she had wings on
her feet. Tía Dolores caught her in her arms.

"There you are, Josefina!" Tía Dolores said.
"I wanted to say good-bye to you."

Josefina pulled back and looked at Tía Dolores's
face. "I'm going to Santa Fe," Tía Dolores said. "I'm
going to see my dear mamá, whom I have not seen
for ten years. But then I'll come back."

"When?" asked Josefina.

Tía Dolores laughed. "Soon," she said. "And
when I come back, I'll stay as long as you need me."

Josefina hugged Tía Dolores hard. Then Tía
Dolores swung herself up onto the wagon.

"Well, well, well," said Abuelito. He pretended
to be cross. "Now it seems that if I want to see
Dolores, I'm going to have to come here and see all
of you girls, too. What a bother! What a bother!"
He sighed. "At least I don't have to carry that piano
with me today. Though if we meet up with any

thieves, I'll just have to frighten them off with my singing, I suppose!"

Then he kissed Josefina and her sisters good-bye and gave them his blessing.

"*Adiós,* Abuelito!" called all the girls as the wagon pulled away. "*Adiós,* Tía Dolores."

"Come back soon!" Josefina sang out as she waved good-bye.

As soon as the wagon was out of sight, Josefina hurried back inside. She went to the kitchen to get a jar. She wanted to fill the jar with water to sprinkle on Mamá's flowers.

Tía Dolores will be back soon, she thought. *I want the flowers to be beautiful when she returns!*

Josefina set off for the stream, whistling Tía Dolores's tune.

Looking
Back
1824

A Peek Into
the Past

America in 1824

This painting shows settlers preparing to build New Mexico's capital city of Santa Fe about 1608. Santa Fe is the oldest capital city in the United States.

Today, New Mexico is one of the 50 states in the United States. But in 1824, when Josefina was a girl, New Mexico was part of the country of Mexico. For hundreds of years before that, all of Mexico—including New Mexico—belonged to Spain. In fact, Spain once ruled huge areas that are now part of the United States. Spanish colonists built many towns and cities that are still important today, such as Los Angeles and San Francisco, California; Santa Fe, New Mexico; and San Antonio, Texas.

Spanish and Mexican settlers first came to New Mexico 400 years

In 1824, the tan area on this map belonged to Mexico. The red line shows the U.S. border today.

Settlers carried their belongings to New Mexico in carts pulled by oxen. The wooden wheels squeaked so loudly they could be heard for miles.

ago, in 1598—even before the Pilgrims landed in Plymouth, Massachusetts. The settlers came to claim land of their own. They built their homes in the mountains and valleys along the Rio Grande, the biggest river in New Mexico. Many New Mexicans today are related to these early settlers.

The small town of Santa Fe was the capital, but most settlers lived in villages and on ranchos. It was difficult to raise crops and animals on the dry, mountainous land. Drought was a constant worry, and so were sudden floods caused by heavy rainstorms. Summers were hot and winters were bitter cold. Lightning, grizzly bears, mountain lions, and rattlesnakes killed farm animals and sometimes people.

To survive, everyone, even children, worked hard. While men and boys worked in the fields or herded animals, women and girls cooked, gardened, and tended the home.

This painting shows a kitchen scene from Josefina's time. One woman is grinding corn using stones called a **mano** and **metate** like the ones shown below the painting. The woman next to her is using cornmeal to make tortillas.

Children like Josefina knew their grandparents, aunts, uncles, and cousins very well. Usually all these relatives lived nearby. Sometimes they lived together in one large household. Orphans, widows, or Indian servants might become part of the family, too.

The settlers brought their language and customs with them to New Mexico. They spoke Spanish, kept their Catholic faith, and enjoyed music and dances from Spain and Mexico. They raised animals that were common in Spain, such as horses, mules, donkeys, oxen, sheep, and chickens. They grew crops that were familiar to them,

Spanish traditions were important to New Mexicans. The settlers made beautiful religious paintings and statues for their churches and homes. On special occasions, they enjoyed lively dances called **fandangos.**

Pueblo Indians in New Mexico wore leather moccasins. The settlers soon began to wear these sturdy, comfortable shoes, too.

such as wheat, onions, carrots, apples, and apricots. To water their fields, they built special ditches called *acequias* much like the ones used in Spain. But they also learned from their Indian neighbors to use native foods like corn, squash, and pine nuts, and to make clothing such as moccasins.

Pueblo Indians had lived in New Mexico for centuries before the settlers arrived. Over the years, the Indians and the settlers slowly learned to live as neighbors. By the time Josefina was a girl, the settlers and the Pueblo Indians often fought together against enemy tribes such as the Comanche, Apache, Navajo, and Ute. These Indians sometimes traveled to northern New Mexico to raid homes and farms. New Mexican settlers never forgot the danger of Indian attacks, and

Pueblo Indians lived in adobe villages in Josefina's time. Some Pueblo people still live in them today.

women and children were not allowed to go far from home alone.

Families like Josefina's, who lived outside of villages or

Houses on New Mexican ranchos were usually built around an open courtyard. Women and girls did much of their work in the courtyard.

towns, built their homes like small fortresses. The high outside walls had only one or two entrances, with heavy gates that could be bolted shut. These homes often had

A lookout tower for defense

a lookout tower, where people could watch for danger. In case of attack, people and animals were gathered inside the walls and the huge gates were locked tight.

People living in New Mexico needed supplies from Mexico. The Camino Real, or Royal Road, was the trail that connected Santa Fe with Mexican towns and cities hundreds of miles south. Most New Mexican traders went as

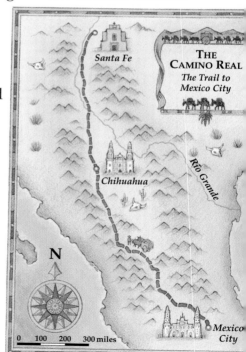

The Camino Real connected Santa Fe with important cities in Mexico. This rugged trail was used by traders, settlers, soldiers, and missionaries.

THE CAMINO REAL
The Trail to Mexico City

Santa Fe

Río Grande

Chihuahua

N

0 100 200 300 miles

Mexico City

New Mexicans wove warm wool blankets like these to use in their homes and to trade for fine things from Mexico.

far as the city of Chihuahua, but a few, like Abuelito, traveled all the way to Mexico City. They brought New Mexican goods such as wool blankets, animal hides, and pine nuts to trade. In return, they received needed items like iron tools and luxuries like chocolate. They also received goods from other countries, such as Chinese silks, spices, and dishes, and European lace, fabrics, and fine jewelry.

Goods from Europe and Asia came to Mexico on great sailing ships. Traders carried luxuries like imported dishes, fine jewelry and hair combs, and painted trunks to New Mexico on the Camino Real.

81

Mule trains like this one carried goods on the Camino Real. This engraving shows men loading up their pack mules to begin another day on the trail.

A caravan like Abuelito's took four or five months to travel from Santa Fe to Mexico City. There were deserts, canyons, mountains, and rivers to cross, and there was always the danger of attack. For more than 200 years the Camino Real was New Mexico's only link to the rest of the world. Then, in 1821, American traders began leading wagon trains from the state of Missouri to New Mexico. They made an important new trade route, which became known as the Santa Fe Trail. For the first time, people and goods from the United States began flowing into New Mexico.

Soldiers traveled with trading caravans on the Camino Real. They helped protect the caravans from danger.

Only 25 years later, in 1846, the United States declared war on Mexico. When the war ended in 1848, America had claimed most of the land that is now the southwestern United States, including California, Nevada, Utah, much of Colorado, and almost all of Arizona and New Mexico.

Although Josefina would never have imagined it when she was nine years old, she would one day be an American—and the cultures and traditions of the New Mexican settlers and their Pueblo neighbors would become part of America, too.

You can see what life was like in Josefina's time by visiting living museums in northern New Mexico. El Rancho de las Golondrinas, near Santa Fe, and La Hacienda de los Martínez in Taos are both restored homes of New Mexican settlers. Above, guides at Las Golondrinas show how settlers preserved chile peppers for the winter.

GLOSSARY OF SPANISH WORDS

Abuelito *(ah-bweh-LEE-toh)*—Grandpa

acequia *(ah-SEH-kee-ah)*—a ditch made to carry water to a farmer's fields

adiós *(ah-dee-OHS)*—good-bye

Camino Real *(kah-MEE-no rey-AHL)*—the main road or trail that ran from Mexico City to New Mexico. Its name means "Royal Road."

fandango *(fahn-DAHNG-go)*—a big celebration or party that includes a lively dance

gracias *(GRAH-see-ahs)*—thank you

gran sala *(grahn SAH-lah)*—the biggest room in the house, used for special events and formal occasions

mano *(MAH-no)*—a stone that is held in the hand and used to grind corn. Dried corn is put on a large flat stone called a *metate*, and then the mano is rubbed back and forth over the corn to break it down into flour.

metate *(meh-TAH-teh)*—a large flat stone used with a *mano* to grind corn

patrón *(pah-TROHN)*—a man who has earned respect because he owns land and manages it well, and is a good leader of his family and his workers

pueblo *(PWEH-blo)*—a village of Pueblo Indians

rancho *(RAHN-cho)*—a farm or ranch where crops are grown and animals are raised

rebozo *(reh-BO-so)*—a long shawl worn by girls and women

sala *(SAH-lah)*—a large room in a house

Santa Fe *(SAHN-tah FEH)*—the capital city of New Mexico. Its name means "Holy Faith."

siesta *(see-ES-tah)*—a rest or nap taken in the afternoon

tía *(TEE-ah)*—aunt

tortilla *(tor-TEE-yah)*—a kind of flat, round bread made of corn or wheat

THE BOOKS ABOUT JOSEFINA

MEET JOSEFINA • An American Girl
Josefina and her sisters are struggling after Mamá's death,
when a surprise gives Josefina hope—and a wonderful idea.

JOSEFINA LEARNS A LESSON • A School Story
Tía Dolores brings exciting changes for Josefina and her
sisters. But will all the changes make them forget Mamá?

JOSEFINA'S SURPRISE • A Christmas Story
A very special Christmas celebration helps Josefina
and her family heal their sadness.

HAPPY BIRTHDAY, JOSEFINA! • A Springtime Story
Josefina faces a terrifying adventure, and her birthday
becomes a celebration of bravery—and second chances.

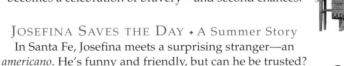

JOSEFINA SAVES THE DAY • A Summer Story
In Santa Fe, Josefina meets a surprising stranger—an
americano. He's funny and friendly, but can he be trusted?

CHANGES FOR JOSEFINA • A Winter Story
Josefina is shocked when Tía Dolores announces that she's
leaving the rancho. Can *anything* persuade her to stay?

◆

WELCOME TO JOSEFINA'S WORLD • 1824
American history is lavishly illustrated
with photographs, illustrations, and
excerpts from real girls' letters and diaries.

MORE TO DISCOVER!

While books are the heart of The American Girls Collection,®
they are only the beginning. The stories in the Collection come
to life when you act them out with the beautiful
American Girls
dolls and their exquisite clothes and accessories.
To request a free catalogue full of things girls love,
send in this postcard, call **1-800-845-0005,**
or visit our Web site at **americangirl.com**.

Please send me an American Girl® catalogue.

My name is ————————————————————————————

My address is ————————————————————————————

City ———————————————— State ——————— Zip ———————
                                                                    3802i

My birth date is ———/———/——— E-mail address ———————————
              month   day   year

Parent's signature ————————————————————————————

And send a catalogue to my friend:

My friend's name is ————————————————————————

Address ————————————————————————————————

City ———————————————— State ——————— Zip ———————
                                                                    1229i

If the postcard has already been removed from this book and you would like to receive an American Girl® catalogue, please send your name and address to:

American Girl
P.O. Box 620497
Middleton, WI 53562-0497

You may also call our toll-free number, **1-800-845-0005,** or visit our Web site at **americangirl.com**.

Place
Stamp
Here

PO BOX 620497
MIDDLETON WI 53562-0497

I.I.I...II.I.I.I..II....I.III....I..II.I.I..I...II.I..I...I..II.I